**London Borough of Hounslow**

Hounslow Library Services

This item should be returned or renewed by the latest date shown. If it is not required by another reader, you may renew it in person or by telephone (twice only). Please quote your library card number. A charge will be made for items returned or renewed after the date due.

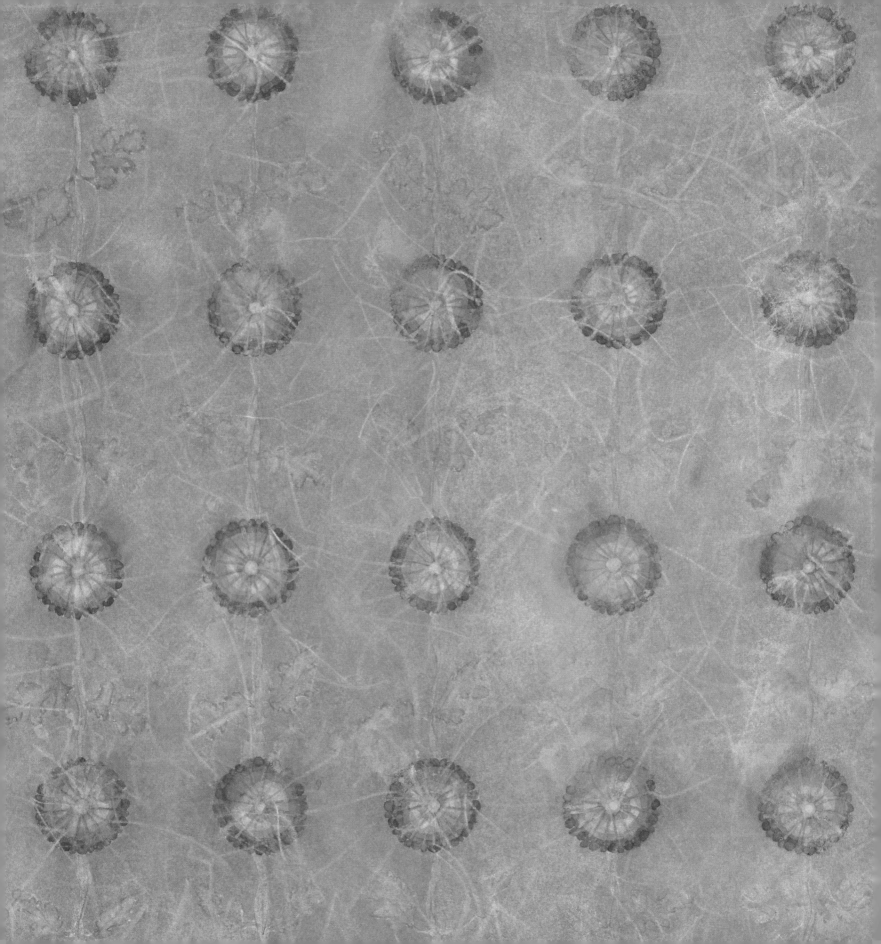

THE NEW GIRL
NICOLA DAVIES
ILLUSTRATIONS CATHY FISHER

This book belongs to

_____

_____

_____

This book is dedicated to all children who struggle to be seen.

With love and thanks to Jackie Morris for kindness, space and time.

Cathy Fisher and Nicola Davies

The New Girl
Published by Graffeg in 2020.
Copyright © Graffeg Limited 2020.

Text copyright © Nicola Davies, illustrations
copyright © Cathy Fisher, design and
production Graffeg Limited.
This publication and content is protected by
copyright © 2020.

Nicola Davies and Cathy Fisher are hereby
identified as the authors of this work in
accordance with section 77 of the Copyrights,
Designs and Patents Act 1988.

A CIP Catalogue record for this book is
available from the British Library.

ISBN 9781913733605

1 2 3 4 5 6 7 8 9

THE NEW GIRL
NICOLA DAVIES
ILLUSTRATIONS CATHY FISHER

GRAFFEG

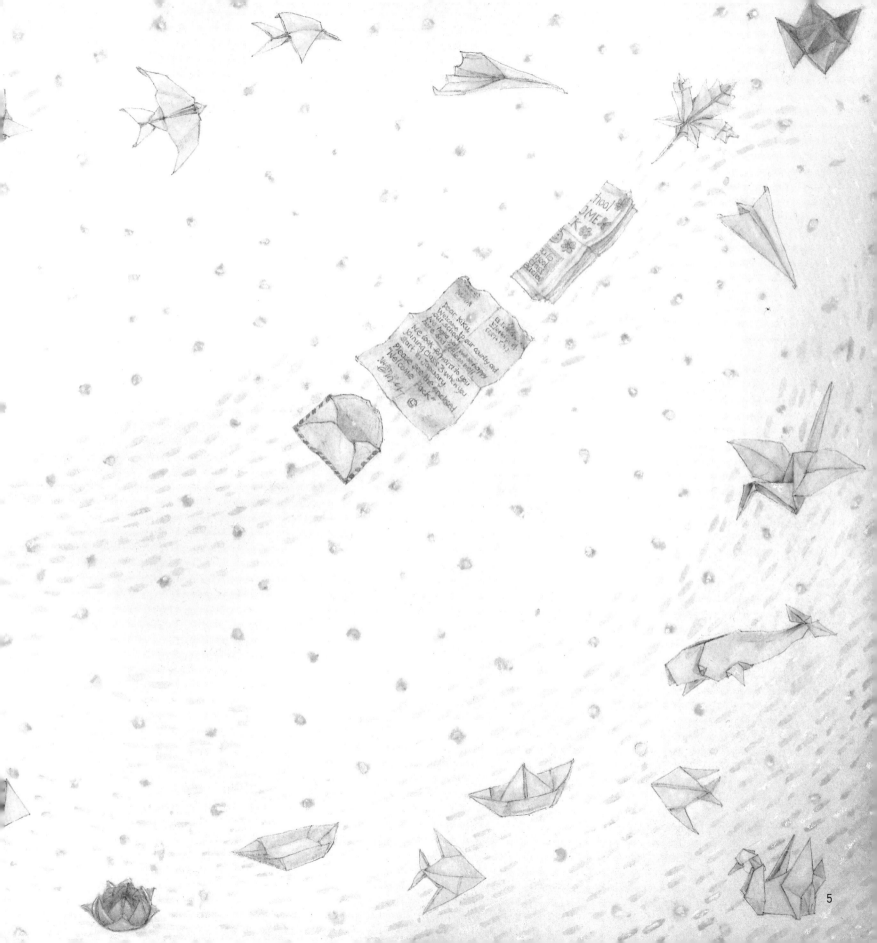

The new girl didn't look like us.
She didn't understand a thing we said,
even when we shouted…

She was wrapped up like a parcel.
We wondered what she hid beneath
those clothes.

Her lunchbox food smelled funny,
so we made her sit apart to eat it.

And at the end of every afternoon she walked away from school, alone.

Every day we laughed at her.

We caught cruelty like a cold that
drew the winter down around us all.

But in the middle of that dark time, a flower came!

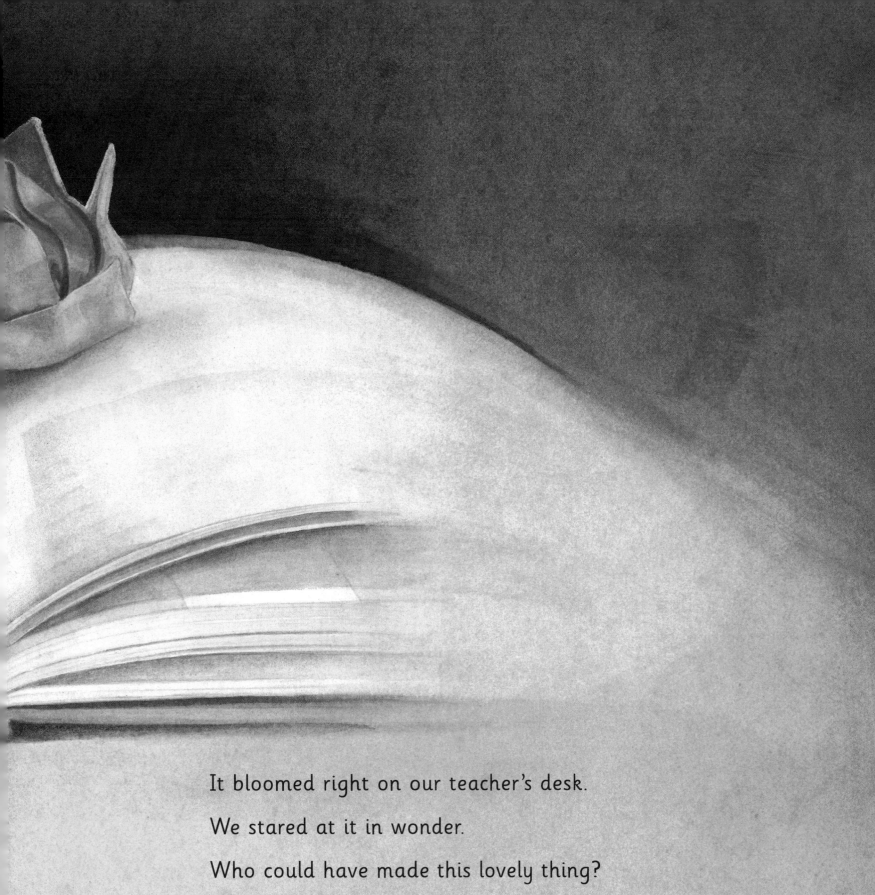

It bloomed right on our teacher's desk.

We stared at it in wonder.

Who could have made this lovely thing?

Every day there was another.

They made us smile.

They made the sun shine in our classroom.

When no more came, we waited,
days and days.

We were so sad.

Our teachers said that we should
try to make our own.

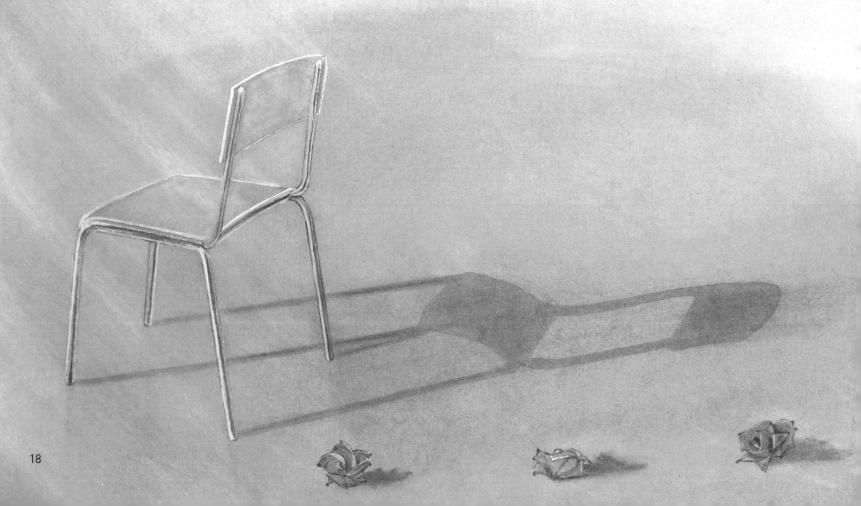

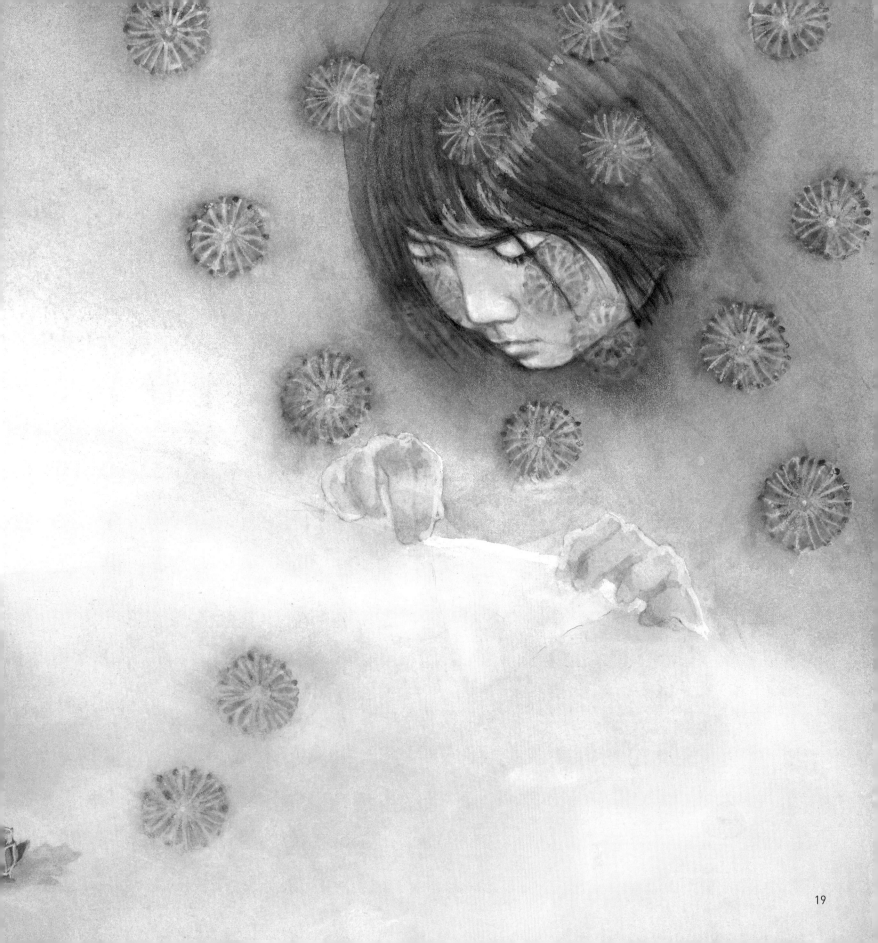

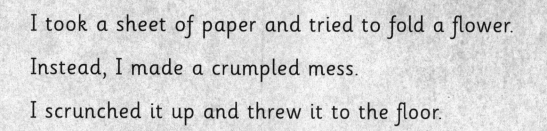

I took a sheet of paper and tried to fold a flower.

Instead, I made a crumpled mess.

I scrunched it up and threw it to the floor.

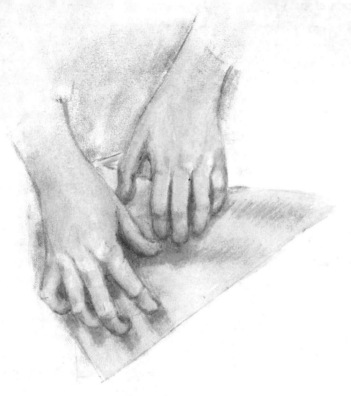

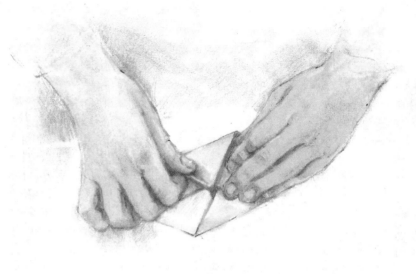

The new girl picked it up.

She smoothed out all my creases.

Then, carefully, with clever fingers, she folded up
a flower and held it out to me.

That day we all learned
how to fold flowers from
a sheet of paper.

We learned their names
in a whole new language,
shobu, akaibara, suiren,
tsubaki, akaichurippu,
iris, rose, lotus, camellia,
tulip, and made a garden!

When I walked home
it wasn't with the
new girl, but with
my friend Kiku...

She is named after a
flower, and made our
classroom bloom.

NICOLA DAVIES

Nicola Davies is an award-winning author whose many books for children include *The Promise* (Green Earth Book Award 2015, Greenaway Shortlist 2015), *Tiny* (AAAS Subaru Prize 2015), *A First Book of Nature* and *Whale Boy* (Blue Peter Award Shortlist 2014). Her titles from Graffeg include *Perfect* (Greenaway Longlist 2017), *The Pond*, *Animal Surprises* (Klaus Flugge Longlist 2017), the Shadows & Light series and the Country Tales series. She graduated in Zoology from King's College, University of Cambridge, and studied geese, bats and whales before becoming a presenter for *The Really Wild Show* and the BBC Natural History Unit. She has been writing for children for more than 20 years. Underlying all Nicola's writing is the belief that a relationship with nature is essential to every human being, and that now, more than ever, we need to renew that relationship.

CATHY FISHER

Cathy Fisher grew up with eight brothers and sisters, playing in the fields overlooking Bath. She has been a teacher and practicing artist all her life, living and working in the Seychelles and Australia for many years. Art is Cathy's first language. As a child she scribbled on the walls of her bedroom and ever since has felt a sense of urgency to paint and draw stories and feelings which she believes need to be heard. *Perfect* (CILIP Kate Greenaway Longlist 2017) was Cathy's first published book, followed by *The Pond* and the Country Tales series.

GRAFFEG CHILDREN'S BOOKS

Perfect
Nicola Davies
Illustrated by Cathy Fisher

The Pond
Nicola Davies
Illustrated by Cathy Fisher

Country Tales series
Nicola Davies
Illustrated by Cathy Fisher
Flying Free
The Little Mistake
A Boy's Best Friend
The Mountain Lamb
Pretend Cows

The White Hare
Nicola Davies
Illustrated by Anastasia Izlesou

Mother Cary's Butter Knife
Nicola Davies
Illustrated by Anja Uhren

Elias Martin
Nicola Davies
Illustrated by Fran Shum

The Selkie's Mate
Nicola Davies
Illustrated by Claire Jenkins

Bee Boy and the Moonflowers
Nicola Davies
Illustrated by Max Low

The Eel Question
Nicola Davies
Illustrated by Beth Holland

The Quiet Music of Gently Falling Snow
Jackie Morris

The Ice Bear
Jackie Morris

The Snow Leopard
Jackie Morris

Queen of the Sky
Jackie Morris

Through the Eyes of Me
Jon Roberts
Illustrated by Hannah Rounding

Through the Eyes of Us
Jon Roberts
Illustrated by Hannah Rounding

Animal Surprises
Nicola Davies
Illustrated by Abbie Cameron

The Word Bird
Nicola Davies
Illustrated by Abbie Cameron

Into the Blue
Nicola Davies
Illustrated by Abbie Cameron

Mouse & Mole series
Joyce Dunbar
Illustrated by James Mayhew
Mouse & Mole
Happy Days for Mouse & Mole
A Very Special Mouse & Mole
Mouse & Mole Have a Party
Mouse & Mole – A Fresh Start

Koshka's Tales – Stories from Russia
James Mayhew

The Knight Who Took All Day
James Mayhew

Gaspard the Fox
Zeb Soanes
Illustrated by James Mayhew

Gaspard – Best in Show
Zeb Soanes
Illustrated by James Mayhew

A Cuddle and a Cwtch
Sarah KilBride
Illustrated by James Munro

Geiriau Diflanedig
Robert Macfarlane
Illustrated by Jackie Morris
Welsh adaptation by
Mererid Hopwood

Fletcher Series
Julia Rawlinson
Illustrated by Tiphanie Beeke
Fletcher and the Springtime Blossom
Fletcher and the Summer Show
Fletcher and the Falling Leaves
Fletcher and the Snowflake Christmas

Molly and the Stormy Sea
Malachy Doyle
Illustrated by Andy Whitson

Molly and the Whale
Malachy Doyle
Illustrated by Andy Whitson

Molly and the Lighthouse
Malachy Doyle
Illustrated by Andy Whitson

Ootch Cootch
Malachy Doyle
Illustrated by Hannah Doyle

Only One of Me – Mum
Lisa Wells and Michelle Robinson
Illustrated by Catalina Echeverri

Only One of Me – Dad
Lisa Wells and Michelle Robinson
Illustrated by Tim Budgen

Monsters Not Allowed!
Tracey Hammett
Illustrated by Jan McCafferty

Celestine and the Hare series
Karin Celestine
Paper Boat for Panda
Small Finds a Home
Honey for Tea
Finding your Place
A Small Song
Catching Dreams
Bertram Likes to Sew
Bert's Garden
Helping Hedgehog Home

Paradise Found
John Milton
Illustrated by Helen Elliott

I Like to Put Food in My Welly
Jason Korsner
Illustrated by Max Low

What Can You See?
Jason Korsner
Illustrated by Hannah Rounding

Ceri & Deri series
Max Low
Good to be Sweet
No Time for Clocks
The Treasure Map
Build a Birdhouse
Young Whippersnapper
The Very Smelly Telly Show

Walking with Bamps
Roy Noble
Illustrated by Karl Davies

The B Team
Roy Noble
Illustrated by Karl Davies

Leap, Hare, Leap!
Dom Conlon
Illustrated by Anastasia Izlesou